MOST VALUABLE PLAYERS

MVP 3

THE **FOOTBALL FUMBLE**

MVP

#1 *The Gold Medal Mess*
#2 *The Soccer Surprise*
#3 *The Football Fumble*
#4 *The Basketball Blowout*

Also by David A. Kelly

The Ballpark Mysteries® series

***Babe Ruth and the
Baseball Curse***

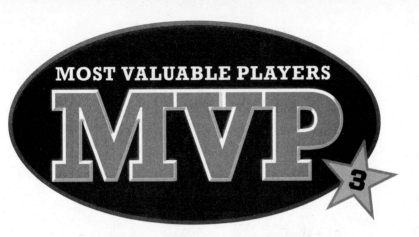

MOST VALUABLE PLAYERS

MVP

3

THE FOOTBALL FUMBLE

David A. Kelly

illustrated by Scott Brundage

A STEPPING STONE BOOK™

Random House 🏠 New York

This book is dedicated to kids who are struggling to learn
how to read. It wasn't easy for me, either. Stick with it because
reading's so much fun once it "clicks" for you.
—D.A.K.

Text copyright © 2016 by David A. Kelly
Cover art and interior illustrations copyright © 2016 by Scott Brundage

All rights reserved. Published in the United States by Random House Children's Books,
a division of Penguin Random House LLC, New York.
Random House and the colophon are registered trademarks and A Stepping Stone Book
and the colophon are trademarks of Penguin Random House LLC.

Visit us on the Web!
SteppingStonesBooks.com
randomhousekids.com

Educators and librarians, for a variety of teaching tools, visit us at RHTeachersLibrarians.com

Library of Congress Cataloging-in-Publication Data is available upon request.

ISBN 978-0-553-51325-7 (pbk.) — ISBN 978-0-553-51326-4 (lib. bdg.) —
ISBN 978-0-553-51327-1 (ebook)

Printed in the United States of America

10 9 8 7 6 5 4 3 2 1

This book has been officially leveled by using the F&P Text Level Gradient™ Leveling System.

Random House Children's Books supports the First Amendment and celebrates the right to read.

CONTENTS

MVP Stats

Meet the MVPs!

MAX

Great athlete—
and a great detective

ALICE

Archery ace
and animal lover

NICO

Can't wait to practice
and can't wait to play

LUKE

Loves to exercise
his funny bone

KAT

Captures the best
game-day moments
on camera

A WINNING STRATEGY!

"Blue twenty-two!" Nico yelled. "Hut, hut, hike!"

Nico snapped the football back to Max. Their friends Alice and Luke counted five-Mississippi and sprang forward. They were trying to grab one of the blue flags hanging from either side of Max's waist before he could pass the ball or run by them.

"Come on, Max!" called Luke's sister, Kat, from the sideline.

Max tucked the ball under his arm and started to run. Alice headed straight for him. Max dodged to the left to get away. But as he did, the ball slipped through his fingers.

"Oh no! It's a fumble!" Kat yelled as the ball bounced end over end down the field. The flag football rules at Franklin Elementary School allowed fumbles, backward passes (or laterals), and a few other plays that made it more like regular football. Just no tackling!

Before Max could recover the football, Alice scooped it up. She tucked it under her arm and zipped down the field. There was no way for Nico or Max to catch up. Alice was a fast runner. A second later, she crossed the goal line.

Touchdown!

Nico's shoulders slumped. He brushed his dark hair back. Nico was one of the best athletes at Franklin Elementary School. He loved playing every kind of sport, but he didn't like losing. He held up his hands and shook them in pretend anger. "Max!" he said. "Not again!"

At the far end of the football field, Alice held the ball up and spiked it into the ground. She pointed at Max and smiled. "Butterfingers!" she called. "Max has butterfingers!"

Max scuffed the field with his shoe. "I'm just tired," he said. "We've been practicing forever!" Max liked reading more than sports. But he loved playing with his friends.

It was Wednesday afternoon. Max, Nico, Luke, Alice, Kat, and the rest of their team had spent an hour practicing football after school. They were getting ready for a big game against Hamilton Elementary School on Saturday.

But after practice had finished, the five friends decided to stay even later to work on a few more plays. Kat was the team's coach.

Kat ran onto the field from the sidelines. The purple ribbons in her curly hair streamed along behind her. She waved her clipboard. "Alice, teasing Max isn't helping!" she yelled. "Everyone come here and huddle up."

Alice ran back as Max, Nico, and Luke huddled with Kat.

"Max, that was a good try, but you've got to hold on to the ball better, like this," Kat said. She took the ball from Alice and tucked it under her right arm. "Use your fingers to hold the front of the ball and press the back of it against your biceps. Then hold it tight against your chest. That way it will be harder to drop. We can't make any mistakes if we want to beat Hamilton."

"The only way we're going to beat Hamilton is if they turn into eggs and someone gives us a whisk," Luke said. He loved to joke, but no one laughed. Luke looked around. "Didn't you get it?" he asked. "Eggs? Beat them?" Still, no one laughed. They were all too tired from practice. Luke shook his head. "It's your loss," he said. "You're missing a good *yolk*!"

Nico groaned. "Oh, that's bad," he said.

"But not as bad as our chance of beating Hamilton," Max said. "Maybe we can figure out a secret plan to win!" Max was big on secrets and special plans. He wanted to be a detective when he grew up, like his father. He had even gone to detective camp last summer.

Kat nodded. "We might need a secret weapon to win. Even with all our practicing, it doesn't look good. Hamilton has won five out of the last six years. It always seems like their players are bigger and better than ours."

"But they're not!" Max said. "Well, they may be bigger than me, but they're in the same grade as us." Max was the smallest one of the group.

"That's not what makes them better than us," Kat said. "They always beat us because they practice so much! They start practicing in the summer for this game. They always have special plays."

Nico clapped his hands together. "That's it! I've got it," he said. "I know how to win Saturday's game against Hamilton! This is a job for the MVP Club!"

Everybody turned to look at him. A little while ago, the five friends had helped save their school Olympics by discovering who was trying to sabotage the games. They were awarded Most Valuable Player medals. After that, the kids had decided to form the MVP Club to play sports and have adventures together.

"How can the MVP Club help Franklin beat Hamilton?" Alice asked.

"It's easy," Nico said. "All we have to do is spy on Hamilton's practice tomorrow after school and learn their plays!"

SPIED!

"Pssst! Kat!" Max whispered. "Keep your head down!"

Kat ducked. It was Thursday afternoon, and she and Max were hiding behind a brick wall outside Hamilton Elementary School. The rest of the MVP Club had voted to send just two members to spy on the team.

"Follow me," Max whispered. "But stay down so we don't get caught! If the Hamilton team knows we're here, they might beat us up or something!"

He led Kat along the wall that ringed

the athletic field behind the school. The Hamilton football team had just come out to practice.

Max and Kat crept along the wall toward the bleachers on the far side of the field. They could hear the calls of Hamilton's quarterback. "Red twenty-four! Red twenty-four! Hut, hut, hike!"

Kat peeked her head over the top of the wall, then motioned for Max to pop up and watch the action. The Hamilton team wore matching football jerseys. The players on offense wore red. The players on defense wore white. They also had matching plastic cleats. They looked a lot more professional than the Franklin team.

The Hamilton quarterback was so large he looked like a middle school kid. Two receivers had run far down the field as their defense tried to stop them. The players around the quarterback blocked the rushers so he had time to make a throw. Two seconds later, the quarter-back saw an opening and let the football fly. It sailed high into the sky and came down right before the end zone. The Hamilton receiver shot to his right and held his arms out. The football dropped into his hands like someone had placed it there. One more step and he crossed the line.

Touchdown!

Kat let out a soft whistle. "Wow!" she whispered. "They look like an NFL team compared to us!"

Max sank down on his heels. "I know," he said. "We need a plan."

Kat tugged his shirt. "Come on," she said. "Once we get to our hiding spot, we can study their plays."

They continued along the outside wall until there was an opening. A few minutes later, Max and Kat had found their way under the shiny silver bleachers. It was dark and damp, but they had a clear view of the field from between the rows of seats.

"This is great!" Kat said. "It's so easy to spy on their practice!"

Max nodded. He pulled a pen and small notebook out of his back pocket. "You watch and tell me what they're doing, and I'll write it down," he said.

For the next half an hour, Kat and Max studied the Hamilton team. They watched as the team ran through one play after the other. Kat would describe the plays, and Max would write them down. Kat also used her phone to take pictures.

Hamilton's quarterback looked good. But one of the other Hamilton players really stuck out. His name was Logan. He was taller and bigger than most of the other players. Even though the quarterback called the plays, Logan kept telling the other players what to do.

"I can't believe you just dropped that

pass!" he yelled at one. "We're not going to win with mistakes like that!"

A few plays later, Logan exploded when one of the smaller Hamilton players didn't run fast enough. "My grandmother runs faster than that!" Logan hollered. "You're out for the next five plays."

The player went and sat on the sidelines while another one took his place.

"Wow, Logan's hard on his teammates," Max said. "That kid *was* running fast."

Kat nodded. "Yeah, he likes picking on people," she said. "It's too bad because Logan actually seems to be a pretty good player."

Hamilton kept practicing. And Logan kept yelling at different teammates. When a player flubbed a handoff, Logan got three other kids to tease him. The three kept dropping the football and pretending to cry. Logan laughed out loud. But it looked like the player who had made the mistake was the one who really wanted to cry.

Shortly after, the football team took a break for water. Max looked over his notes. He had written down a bunch of Hamilton's plays and formations and taken notes on the different players.

"They're a really good team, even if Logan's mean," Kat said.

Max nodded. "They are definitely better than us," he said. He looked at the notebook in his hands. Max thought for a moment, and then his eyes lit up.

"But we're a good team, too," he said. "And more importantly, they're not perfect! They make mistakes just like us. And Logan's big, but he's a bully. I think we can win!"

Max tapped the notebook against

the back of his hand. Then he threw the notebook into the dirt.

"What did you do that for?" Kat asked. She leaned over and picked it up.

"You know, we *are* a good team. Too good to be doing this," Max said. "We need to win because we did our best. Not because we spied and cheated."

Kat looked at Max for a moment. Then she nodded. "Yeah, you're right," she said. "This seemed like a good idea, but we're better than this. Let's rip up the notes and leave!"

Max took the notebook back. Then he pulled out the pages he had written on and tore them all up. He tossed them into a nearby trash can. Kat deleted the pictures she had taken.

"Let's get out of here," Max said.

Kat nodded. They slipped out from under the bleachers and tried to sneak around to the other side of the brick wall.

"Hey, stop them!" called out one of the Hamilton players. Max and Kat froze. They'd been spotted! "They've been spying on our practice!"

The players on the Hamilton team started to run toward Max and Kat!

"Quick!" Kat said. They scrambled around the brick wall and ran for their bikes.

Right before they reached the bike rack, a red-and-white blur jumped over the brick wall. It landed on the ground directly in front of them.

It was one of the Hamilton football players!

He crouched down like he was going to tackle them. Max and Kat skidded to a halt.

"Trying to steal our plays?" he asked. "You two must be from Franklin. But you won't be going back there."

He smacked a fist into his palm. The rest of the Hamilton football team rounded the corner of the brick wall. They were coming from behind!

"Go to the right!" Max yelled to Kat.

Max shot to the left of the football player, while Kat shot to the right. They were both just out of reach. The football player didn't know which one to grab for, so he lunged forward and missed them both! Max and Kat zipped past him.

The football player fell to the ground as Max and Kat jumped on their bikes. They wheeled them around and pedaled with all their might.

The rest of the Hamilton team ran after them. But a minute later, when Max and Kat zoomed around the corner to another street, the football players were far behind.

It had been close, but Max and Kat had escaped!

DISASTER!

"Oof!" Luke grunted as his elbow bumped into a door. A pile of soccer balls, kick balls, and volleyballs slipped through his arms.

THUMP! THUMP! THUMP! THUMP!

The balls bounced all over the school hallway. Luke scrambled after them.

"I can't believe you volunteered us to do this, Kat," he said. Luke scooted around and picked up the balls. "We should be out on the field with the rest of the football team. This is one of our last practices before the big game on Saturday!"

"I know, but I promised Ms. Suraci we'd get this done today," Kat said. Ms. Suraci was Franklin's PE teacher. "We can go out there as soon as we move all the sports balls from the gym to the new supply closet in the hallway. When I told Ms. Suraci last week that we could do the project, I didn't know we'd have football practice on the same day!"

It was Friday afternoon, and the MVP Club had been working on Ms. Suraci's project since school ended.

Max picked up four balls from the pile and started to trudge toward the new supply room. "This is going to take forever," he said.

Luke nudged Max's shoulder as he walked by. "But just think," Luke said. "If it *did* take forever, then at least we wouldn't lose the big football game tomorrow! See, there's a bright side to helping Ms. Suraci!"

Max groaned. "Luke, maybe we'd be

able to win if you spent less time joking and more time thinking about the game," he said.

"Well, if you hadn't run away from the Hamilton practice, we'd have all their plays and be able to beat them easily!" Luke said. He and Nico pulled out more balls from the closet.

"Hey, Max and I decided that we wanted to win fair and square," Kat said. "That's why we tore up the notes and left."

Luke snickered. "Really? It sounded like you left because *you* were going to get torn up!"

"Okay, we did have to leave in a hurry," Kat said. "But Hamilton is the one that's going to get torn up on the field tomorrow! We just have to stick together and do our best. Even if they're a better team, I know we can find a way to win."

Nico dropped his load of balls in the supply closet. His shoulders slumped.

"We're not going to find it in here," he said. He pointed to his blue football jersey that read *Franklin Football* on the front. "We need to be outside practicing."

Kat watched as Nico, Luke, Alice, and Max carried balls from the gym to the hallway.

"Hey! I've got an idea," she said. "It's not exactly football, but maybe we can practice *and* find a way to finish this job more quickly!"

She had everyone finish up with the load of balls they had. Then she pulled and pushed each one of them into a different spot. She put Alice inside the gym's closet. Then she put Nico about ten feet away in the center of the gym. He had a clear view down the school hallway. She put Max halfway down the hallway, near the new supply closet. Finally, she put Luke inside the supply closet.

"Hey, are you giving me a time-out?" Luke asked. "Because if you are, I'm going to sit down and throw a temper tantrum!" He winked at his friends.

Kat rolled her eyes at her brother and shook her head. "No, you're going to help get the job done quickly so we can practice for the game! Watch this!"

Kat headed back to the gym. On the way, she whispered to Max, Nico, and Alice. Then she stood to the side, put two fingers in her mouth, and gave a sharp whistle.

TWEET!

Alice picked up a ball from the gym closet. She tossed it sideways to Nico. Nico easily caught the ball and immediately threw it down the long hallway to Max. Max grabbed the ball and ran it into the new supply closet, where Luke stacked it up.

Kat's plan worked like a charm! For the next fifteen minutes, Kat coached the group as Alice tossed one ball after another backward to Nico, who then threw long passes down the hall to Max. Max ran them inside the supply closet and stacked them with Luke.

In almost no time, they had finished the project for Ms. Suraci. They closed the closet doors, burst out the side door of the school, and ran over to where the rest of the football team was practicing.

Practice was half over. To help the team, a group of sixth graders from the middle school had agreed to scrimmage against them. But the Franklin football team wasn't doing well. They had been struggling to score against the sixth graders. Franklin had only scored once, while the sixth graders had scored five times!

"It's going to be a tough game," said one of the older boys. "We played Hamilton a couple of years ago and got crushed. They're really good."

Kat picked up her clipboard on the sidelines and whistled for everyone to huddle. They listened as Kat outlined a few plays to try, and then they started the second half of the practice. Nico played quarterback. The rest of them took turns playing defense or running for passes.

Unfortunately, the rest of the practice didn't go as well as Ms. Suraci's project. Nico was a good quarterback. But even though he was able to throw the ball well, the Franklin team wasn't very good at catching it. Kat had the team run all types of plays, but nothing seemed to work quite right.

When the practice broke up half an hour later, the MVP Club walked away with their heads low.

"I don't know how we're going to win tomorrow," Kat said. "We'll need some magic in order to beat Hamilton."

COLD CONFRONTATION

"Hey, I know something magic that will help us win," Luke said.

The others looked up eagerly. "What?" Alice asked. "Do you have a new formation we can use?"

Luke laughed. "No, it's even better than that," he said.

"Great!" Nico said. He jumped up and down and did a cartwheel. He loved to put his gymnastics skills to use.

"Well, what is it?" Alice asked.

The rest of the MVP Club looked at

Luke. They waited for his magic solution for beating Hamilton.

"Ice cream!" he yelled. "Let's go to Annabelle's Ice Cream. It'll be strengthening! Football is all about strategy and plans. All we have to do is feel good about ourselves and plan to win, and we'll be fine tomorrow!"

They were quiet while Luke's idea sank in.

"Yay! That's a great idea!" Kat said. "We'll be the *coolest* football team around!"

Nico gave Luke a high five. "Last one there pays!" he said, and took off running. The rest of the MVP Club ran after him.

As usual, Nico came in first. Max came in last.

"Aww, come on," Max said as they stepped into Annabelle's. "I don't really have to pay, do I?"

Kat laughed. "No, Max," she said. "Nobody agreed to that except Nico. And Nico only said it because he knew he'd be first!"

One after another, they ordered their cones. Luke got banana ripple with extra sprinkles. Max got chocolate chocolate chip. Kat ordered mint mango. Alice picked blueberry pie. And Nico ordered maple bacon waffle.

After getting their ice cream, the group sat at the tables at the front of the store. Annabelle's was on Main Street, so the kids could watch cars go by as they licked their treats.

When they were halfway done with their ice cream, Nico spotted something. He pointed across the street. "It's the Hamilton football team!"

Max and Kat looked at each other. "Uh-oh," Max said. The Hamilton team was headed straight for Annabelle's!

Max shifted to a chair farther away from the door.

"Ignore them," Kat said. "We're just having ice cream. Let's not get into trouble!"

The kids from Hamilton crossed the street. When they got to Annabelle's, a tall kid in front noticed Nico's Franklin Football shirt.

"Hey, look," he said. "It's some of the Franklin football team. They might as well *lick* their ice cream, because we're going to *lick* them in the game tomorrow!"

Nico gritted his teeth and shifted in his chair. Kat gave him a stare that said to *stay still.* Nico nodded and took a deep breath.

"Yeah, it'll be like playing against a bunch of ants!" another Hamilton player said.

Kat stood up. She was just a few feet from the Hamilton kids.

"Come on, team," she said. "Let's get

going. We can settle this on the field."

The rest of the MVP Club stood up. As they started to leave, one of the Hamilton players stepped forward. It was Logan, the player Max and Kat had seen the day before. He was in front of Max. Logan reached out and tried to shove Max, but Max jumped to the right.

"No, not ants," Logan said. "Rabbits! Look at this one! He's small and has big ears, just like a rabbit."

Logan took another step toward Max. Max backed up into Alice.

"And look how he jumps away!" Logan said. "We can call him Hopper! Come here, Hopper!"

"Good one, Logan!" called another Hamilton player.

Logan leaned toward Max and sneered. "I can't wait to see you on the football field tomorrow, Hopper," he said. "I bet if we leave a pile of carrots on the sideline, you'd just sit and nibble them rather than play football!"

The Hamilton team burst out laughing. Max's ears burned. He clenched his fists and started toward Logan, but Alice pulled him back.

"Don't let them bother you, Max," she said. "They're bullies. Wait until the football game. We'll show them."

But Logan was just getting started. He held his hands in front of him like a bunny and hopped around in a circle. "Hey, Hopper," he said. "Maybe you can bring us some treats in a basket. Do you have any candy for us? Or something sweet?"

Logan stuck out his top teeth and made bunny sounds with his mouth. "Tuc-tuc-tuc-tuc," he said. "Tuc-tuc-tuc."

The Hamilton team laughed. "Maybe he's got an egg for you, Logan!" one of them called.

Logan stepped closer to Max. He leaned right up to Max's face and stared threateningly at him. "Yeah, you got an egg for me, little rabbit?" he asked.

Kat pushed her way from behind Max and stepped in between him and Logan. "No, he doesn't," she said. "But I do!"

Kat held up her blueberry pie ice cream cone. Logan looked at it for a moment and raised an eyebrow. Small drops of blue ice cream dripped on his shoes.

"You want something sweet?" she asked. "Here you go, you big bully!"

Kat smooshed her cone right into Logan's forehead!

The cone stuck to Logan's head for a moment. It made Logan look a little bit like a unicorn. The Franklin kids cheered and burst out laughing.

Logan looked stunned. But he returned to normal a second later, when

Kat's ice cream cone dropped to the ground with a splat.

Logan wiped his forehead with the back of his arm. He sneered at Kat and waved for his friends to follow him.

"You think that's funny, but we'll be the ones laughing tomorrow!" he called over his shoulder. "Your team doesn't have a chance."

HELP FROM NEW YORK CITY

The Franklin football team gathered at school early Saturday morning for one final practice before the big game.

Like the practices earlier in the week, the team tried one play after another, but nothing worked. Nico's passes were too long or too short. Receivers got confused on their routes. The players couldn't even keep their signals straight. Finally, Kat blew her whistle and waved her clipboard.

"Time to take a break!" she called. "Let's get our heads in the game!"

While the team rested, the MVP Club gathered under a tree on the sidelines. Nico drank some water, while Alice lay on her back and looked up at the sky. Max picked up a stick from the ground and started whacking at the grass with it. He was thinking of ways to get back at Logan. Luke was joking, of course. He stumbled around with his arms up over his head.

"All the players on the Hamilton team were huge!" Luke said. "They were like giants!"

Kat rolled her eyes. "They weren't any bigger than us, Luke," she said. "They were just meaner. But that's not going to matter. We've just got to find a way to play smarter than them. Football is all about strategy."

Max held his stick in front of him, with his hands at either end. "My strategy is to get back at Logan," he said.

"I know I'm small and my ears are big. But maybe I can find a way to break him like *this*!"

Max twisted his hands downward.
SNAP!
His stick broke in half.

"That would show him," Max said. He flung the pieces over his shoulder.

"Um, Max?" Luke asked. "Even if you could snap Logan in half like that stick, that's not the solution. Plus, he's still bigger than you!"

Max let out a sigh. "I know," he said. "Maybe I could figure out a way to outsmart him or something."

Luke nodded. "Hey, I've got an idea," he said. "What if I distract Logan right before the Hamilton quarterback calls hike? Then, while he's looking at me, you tie his shoes together! When the play starts, he'll fall flat on his face!"

Luke pretended that his shoes were stuck together. He wobbled back and forth, then held out his hands and fell forward with a plop!

Max laughed. "Great idea!" he said. "We'll see how he likes that!"

Kat shook her head and tapped her

clipboard with a pen. "That's not going to work," she said. "Ignore Logan. He's a bully. Maybe he's mean to everyone because he doesn't have any friends."

"Or maybe he's just mean," Max said. "I don't like him."

"You don't have to like him," Alice said. "We have to find a way to beat him! He won't think you're small when you win."

"You know, being small can be a big advantage sometimes," Kat said. "You just have to play to your strengths. Don't let Logan rattle you. We'll find a way."

"Yeah. Okay. Let's take a break from football for a while," Max said. "I don't want to think about Logan anymore."

"Good idea," Kat said. "Luke and I have to tell you about our trip to Washington, D.C.! We went to the top of the Washington Monument. And then we visited the Lincoln Memorial. That's the statue of Abraham Lincoln sitting in a chair. It's huge!"

Luke clapped his hands together. "That's it!" he said. "All we have to do is get that giant Abraham Lincoln to play on our team. We'd win for sure!"

Luke jumped up and slowly stomped around the grass like he was a huge Abraham Lincoln playing football.

"Four score and this Saturday, we set forth to demolish Hamilton on the field of football," Luke said solemnly. "They were a better team and they would have won, but I squished them all like bugs under my giant stone feet!" *CRUNCH! CRUNCH! CRUNCH! CRUNCH!*

The group laughed as Luke stomped around.

But Max didn't. He was thinking.

"Hang on," Max said. "I've got an idea. I have to go to the library!"

"Now is a funny time to remember your overdue library book!" Nico called.

Max ran inside the school. He returned a few minutes later and tossed a book on the grass. The cover said *Football Fundamentals.*

Nico sneered at the book. "We don't need books to win. We just need more practice!" he said.

Max shook his head. "No, all that

talk about vacations got me thinking about a trip we took to New York City," he said. "We saw the Statue of Liberty. It was huge! It's a lot bigger than Abraham Lincoln is. We went way up high inside the Statue of Liberty. We could see for miles!"

Luke pretended to be the Statue of Liberty. He held his right arm up like he was holding a torch. And he tucked his left arm in front of him like he was holding a tablet.

Everyone looked at Max. "Um, okay," Nico said. "So you saw the Statue of Liberty. Who cares? We have a football game to win."

Max grinned. "That's just it! We're going to use the Statue of Liberty to win the game!" Max opened the football book. He flipped to a chapter titled "Trick Plays" and pointed to the first one. It was called the Statue of Liberty.

"See? Trick plays can be an important part of football games," Max said. "And one of the most famous is the Statue of Liberty play. The quarterback pretends to throw the ball, and instead hands it off to a runner, who sweeps up the side of the field away from the defense. Lots of teams have used it!"

"Why is it called the Statue of Liberty?" Luke asked.

Max grabbed the football. He raised his arm up and held the football back over his shoulder. His other arm was at his side.

"When I pretend to throw the ball, it makes me look a little like the Statue of Liberty holding her torch," he said. "After I fake a throw, I secretly hand the ball off to someone on our team. They take it and run. The other team keeps waiting for a pass that never happens!"

"Cool," Nico said. "Let's give it a try!"

"That's great, Max," Kat said. She picked up the football book and pointed at it. "You might not be bigger than Logan, but you're smarter!"

The kids put on their uniforms, ran out to the field, and took their positions.

"New York! Washington! Vacation!" Nico called out. "Hut, hut, hike!"

Luke snapped the ball to Nico. Nico pretended to throw it, but instead slipped it to Alice as she swept around behind him. She zipped up the field and spiked the ball in the end zone.

The Statue of Liberty play worked like a charm!

HARD TIME AT HALFTIME

"Come on, team! Let's go!" Kat called half an hour later. "It's game time!"

She blew her whistle, and the Franklin team sprinted over to the main football field next to the school. The day was sunny and perfect for a game of flag football. A slight breeze blew across the field. Hamilton was huddled on the other side of the field. Parents of kids from each team had gathered along the sidelines as well.

Each of the Franklin players strapped on a white belt. Then they attached a strip of blue fabric to the sticky area on each side of their waists. The "flags" hung down the sides of their legs. During the game, the Hamilton players would try to rip one of the flags off the player carrying the ball. Once a flag was ripped off, the player was down and the play was over. Five players from each team were allowed on the field.

The referee walked out to the center of the field and blew his whistle. Kat and Max jogged out to meet the coach and a player from the Hamilton team for the coin toss. Whichever team won the coin toss would start with the ball from its own five-yard line. Teams had four downs to advance the ball twenty yards. If they did, the team would get four more downs. Otherwise, the other team would get the ball. Field goals and kicking the ball were not allowed.

When they got to the center of the

field, Max reached out to shake the hand of the Hamilton player. But it was Logan!

Logan moved in close to Max and looked down at him. He spoke quietly so the coach wouldn't hear. "Aww, its Hopper! The wittle bunny came to play football." Logan stuck out his upper teeth and made rabbit sounds at Max. "Tuc-tuc-tuc!"

Max's ears burned red. He drew up his shoulders and stared directly at Logan. Logan stared back at Max.

Max stuck out his hand to shake. Logan's lip twitched. Finally, he reached out and shook Max's hand.

"You can call the coin toss," he said. "But it's not going to matter, because you're going to lose, Hopper!" Logan gave a short laugh.

Max shrugged. "Okay, we'll take heads," he said. "And I wouldn't be so sure about winning!"

The referee flipped a quarter up in the air. It somersaulted end over end until the referee caught it and swatted it onto the back of his other hand.

It was heads! Max and the Franklin team would get the ball first.

"Okay, let's go!" the referee said.

"It's a forty-minute game split into two twenty-minute halves. Teams get six points for each touchdown. No extra points. No tackling. Fumbles and laterals are allowed."

TWEET!

The referee blew his whistle, and the players and coaches jogged back to their sides.

The teams huddled and then ran out to take the field. Since Franklin had the ball first, their offense lined up at their five-yard line.

"Hut, hut, hike!" Nico called. Alice snapped the ball to him, and the Franklin team spread out. Three Hamilton players counted five-Mississippi and then rushed Nico. Luke and Alice tried to block the Hamilton players from getting to him. Max ran down the field so Nico could throw the football to him.

But before Max could get open for the pass, Logan broke through the Franklin defense and headed straight for Nico. Thinking quickly, Nico threw the ball toward Alice. But the ball sailed over her head and bounced on the ground. Incomplete!

"Come on, Nico! Focus!" Kat called from the sideline.

The Franklin team lined up for the second down. Again, Alice snapped the ball to Nico. The players ran their routes. Max sprinted down the sideline, past his defender, and waved his arm at Nico. This time, Max was open. Nico cocked his arm back and threw the football. It spiraled down the field and dropped right into Max's hands!

Max tucked the ball next to his chest and took off running. The Hamilton players scrambled after him. Max passed the thirty-yard line. Then the twenty-yard line. Then the ten. Then he crossed into the end zone.

Touchdown!

The Franklin side erupted in cheers! Parents and players went wild, while the Hamilton team shuffled back to huddle.

It was just a few minutes into the

game and Franklin was ahead 6–0.

But Franklin's lead didn't last long. On the very next play, Hamilton ran the ball all the way down the field for a touchdown. This time, the Hamilton parents and players cheered, while the Franklin players huddled with Kat.

The game was tied, 6–6.

Franklin fought back the next time they had possession of the ball. They tried to move the ball down the field, but the Hamilton players were too good. They covered the Franklin receivers like glue and pulled the flags off the Franklin runners before they could score again.

As the game continued, Franklin couldn't get close to scoring. But Hamilton did. Twice they got near the end zone before Franklin was able to stop them.

"They're blocking everything we try!" Luke said during Franklin's next huddle. "It's like they can tell what we're going to do before we do it."

Nico nodded. "I know," he said. "Let's try the up-the-middle play we practiced yesterday. Come on! Let's go!" Nico clapped his hands, and the Franklin team lined up.

But that play didn't work either.

Hamilton stopped each Franklin play before they could gain any more yards. Soon Hamilton took possession of the ball. Time was running out in the first half, and Hamilton was able to get close to Franklin's end zone.

In two downs, Hamilton did what Franklin couldn't. They scored again! Now Hamilton was up 12–6. The Franklin team was getting desperate.

"This is it," Nico said as they huddled. "We can only try one more play before halftime. Let's do Max's special Statue of Liberty play and tie this game up now! Alice, snap the ball on the word *vacation.*" Nico put his hand out. The rest of the team put their hands on top of his. "On the count of three," Nico said. "One, two, three!"

The pile of hands exploded upward. *"Go, Franklin!"* the team yelled. The players ran to their positions.

Hamilton lined up opposite the Franklin team.

"Blue twenty-two! Yellow. Green. Tangerine!" Nico called. "Washington! New York! Vacation!"

Alice snapped the ball to Nico. Franklin players blocked the Hamilton defense.

Nico dropped back a few steps. He held the ball up high like he was going to pass. He pretended to throw the ball. But he didn't let go of it. As he brought his hand down, he slipped the ball to Max, who had run behind him. Max swept out to the right. The Hamilton team was focused on Nico and didn't seem to be following Max.

It looked like the trick play was going to work!

But then one of the Hamilton players yelled, "Hey, he's got the ball!" A big player zipped across the field to cut Max off. Max dodged to the left, but Logan was there. He was stuck!

Max tried to shift the other way, but he slipped and stumbled. Logan dove and ripped Max's blue flag off! Max was down. The play was over.

Logan looked at Max and made

a face. "Oh, wook at the poor wittle bunny wabbit. He slipped and messed up," Logan said in a baby voice. "Why don't you get up and hop along back to the other baby bunnies?"

As the other Hamilton players laughed, the referee blew his whistle.

TWEET!

The half was over. Max's trick play had failed. Franklin was still behind by six points!

OUT OF GAS

"Argh!" Max said during the halftime break. "I can't believe I blew it!"

"At least you tried!" Alice said. "Don't worry, it's not you. Hamilton's a good team."

"I can't stand Logan," Max said. "I want to get back at him, but he's bigger than me."

Kat shook her head. "Max, we don't have to be bigger to win the game. We just have to be smarter. We need to find something that will give us an edge."

A bunch of the players sat on the

bench, eating oranges and drinking water. Nico went over to a duffel bag he had brought and pulled out a bunch of plastic bags filled with snack mix. He passed them around to the team. Luke took a big handful, popped it in his mouth, and started munching. "This is good!" he said.

"Maybe it will give us an edge," he said. "It's my special snack mix. I call it Nico's Nibbles. It has wasabi peas, bran flakes, sesame sticks, and some dried ginger for zing."

"Ugh!" Luke gasped. He turned to the side and spit a big wad of Nico's snack mix into the dirt. "Peas? I don't like peas!" He grabbed his water bottle and took a big gulp. "Nico, next time you try to poison us, please tell us beforehand!"

Nico laughed. "Peas aren't poison, Luke," he said. "And you liked it before you knew what was in it!"

Luke swallowed his water. "What I'd really like is to find a way to beat Hamilton," he said. He pointed across the field. The other team was laughing and joking around on the bench.

Kat tapped her clipboard. "Gather around," she said. "I can show you why they feel so good about the game."

Everyone formed a circle around Kat. She took out a tablet and pulled up a bunch of pictures. She loved to take photos. She often stayed after school to work on special projects with the art teacher.

"I took some pictures and videos during the game," she said. "They can help us study the types of formations they use and what we can do to beat them."

For the next five minutes, Kat showed the team the pictures and videos. She pointed out where the Franklin team could do better and some of the plays that Hamilton had used against them.

When she was finished, there was still time before the second half. Max pulled out the football book he had gotten from the library and flipped through it.

"Should we try another trick play?" he asked. "There are so many great ones in here. There's the fumblerooski, the hook and ladder, the flea flicker, and the end around. Maybe we could do one and score again!"

Nico shook his head. "We can't," he said. "We haven't practiced any of them. Instead of scoring again, we'd probably lose the ball or something!"

Kat agreed. "I think it's too late to try something we haven't practiced," she said.

A few minutes later, the referee blew the whistle. It was time for the second half!

Both teams ran out to the field. Hamilton had the ball first but wasn't able to score. When Franklin got the ball, Nico took the snap and handed it off to Max for a running play. Max tucked the ball under his arm and barreled forward.

He left the Hamilton players behind as he ran down the field. The only thing that stood between him and the end zone was Logan, who had been playing far back.

Logan ran straight for Max. When he got close, Logan lunged for Max's flag. Max shifted to the left. But Logan shifted, too. Max dodged to the right, but Logan moved in front of him.

Logan smiled. It was clear he had Max stopped.

"Aw, wook at the wittle bunny. He can't go weft and he can't go wight," Logan said. "Poor wittle bunny is going to cry!" Logan balled up his hands and held them to his eyes like he was crying.

Max cradled the ball under his arm. He recalled what Kat had said about being smarter than the Hamilton team. His eyes darted around the field. None of the other Franklin players were open.

There wasn't anything Max could do.

But then Logan's fake crying got his attention. As Logan pretended to rub his eyes, Max spotted an opening.

He ran forward and dove between Logan's legs! Before Logan could stop him, Max tucked and rolled into a somersault and popped up running on the other side of Logan!

He was free and clear. There were no other Hamilton players nearby!

Logan whipped around, but it was too late. Max was almost at the end zone!

Max ran as fast as he could. He didn't look back. Max scored!

The Franklin team and their parents exploded in cheers! The game was tied, 12–12! Kat went wild on the sideline and danced around with her clipboard.

"Way to use your head, Max!" she called. "What a great idea! That'll show those bullies!"

Logan seemed stunned by Max's move. And the rest of the Hamilton team didn't look happy with Logan. The Hamilton player that had flubbed a handoff during practice even yelled out from the sideline, "Hey, Logan! Maybe if *you'd* been focused on the game instead of making fun of him, he wouldn't have scored on you!"

"Yeah, nice job," said another one of the Hamilton players who Logan had teased during practice. "I guess *we're* not the only ones who aren't perfect!"

Logan shook his head and kicked at the ground. He shuffled over to the bench for a drink of water.

When the game resumed, Logan was definitely more quiet and focused, and it was working. He was determined to win. Franklin's lucky score didn't put Hamilton out of the game. Just like the first half, the Hamilton team regrouped quickly. They drove the ball down the field, but Alice blocked a pass on fourth down to prevent them from scoring.

"Woo-hoo, Alice!" Kat called. "Keep it up!"

As the second half went on, both

teams became even more serious. Logan wasn't taunting Max anymore or talking like a baby. He was focused on finding ways to beat Franklin. And Nico and the Franklin team were trying everything they had practiced over the previous week. But neither team scored. As the minutes ticked away, the game remained tied.

Franklin moved the ball down the field with a combination of running and passing plays. Their strategy seemed to be working. As they huddled before the fourth down, Nico ran through the plays they could try. He suggested that they try Max's Statue of Liberty play again.

"It almost worked the first time," Nico said. "And we're only fifteen yards from the end zone. But this time, let's have Alice be quarterback and I'll run the ball."

Everyone nodded. "Great idea," Luke said. "Let's do it!"

The Franklin team lined up. Max acted as the center and snapped the ball to Alice. She dropped back, and at just the right time, Nico ran behind her. She pretended to throw the ball but slipped it into Nico's hands. He took off like a streak up the right side of the field.

The play worked perfectly! The players from Hamilton were focused on Alice, and most of them didn't see Nico get the ball. By the time they did, it was too late. Nico had already zipped past them!

But he hadn't made it past everyone. Logan was near Hamilton's end zone. As Nico ran up the field, Logan spotted him and ran over to intercept him. As they approached each other, Nico tried to stop and run to the left. But Logan was already there.

Nico wasn't able to slow down in time. He and Logan bumped arms. The football sailed out of Nico's hand!

It bounced on the ground and rolled around.

Fumble!

A FLICKER OF HOPE

The football rolled end over end along the ground. Nico and Logan scrambled after it. Nico almost snatched it off the ground, but Logan got there first. His big hands scooped the football up. Hamilton had the ball!

Nico thought fast and grabbed the red flag hanging from Logan's belt. He pulled it off.

Logan was down, but Franklin had lost the ball and the chance to score! Now they would have to keep Hamilton from scoring.

Nico kicked the ground and headed back to the rest of the team. If Hamilton scored, Franklin wouldn't have much time left to tie the game.

"That wasn't your fault," Max said when Nico joined the team's huddle.

Nico's shoulders slumped. He wasn't used to losing. "I should have held on tighter," he said.

Kat stepped forward. "It's not over, and Hamilton hasn't won," she said. "Let's focus on how we can win the game now."

Kat ran through the defensive positions she wanted them to take. A minute later, both teams were back on the field.

On the first snap, Hamilton was able to gain some yards. They quickly set up for another play and completed a pass to gain a few more yards. On third down, a Hamilton player was able to sidestep Alice and gain some ground before Max

tugged his flag off. Hamilton was getting close to the Franklin end zone! On the final down, Logan made a run for the goal line, but Alice grabbed his flag at the ten-yard line. Now Franklin had possession.

With the game almost over and the score tied, Franklin finally had the ball. One touchdown and they would win the game!

"Yahoo!" Nico yelled as the team huddled. "This is it!"

"But we only have about a minute to get the ball all the way down the field!" Max said. "That's going to be really hard."

TWEET!

The referee's whistle blew. Kat had called a time-out. The team ran to the sideline.

Kat pulled out Max's library book. She tapped the cover as the team surrounded her. "I was looking through

Max's book, and I found a new trick play to try!" she said.

"But we haven't had any time to practice it!" Nico said.

Kat smiled. "That's the best part," she said. "We *did* practice it!"

"We've already done the Statue of Liberty twice," Nico said. "They'll be looking for it again."

"It's not the Statue of Liberty!" Kat said. She flipped the book open to the trick plays chapter and tapped the flea flicker page. "The flea flicker is a famous trick play that a lot of teams have done," Kat said.

She explained how it worked. A football team does the flea flicker to fool the other team into thinking they're going to run the ball when they're actually going to pass it. It's like the opposite of the Statue of Liberty play, which looked like a pass but was actually a run.

"Nico, you take the snap, and then

hand it off to a runner," Kat said. "The runner then heads to the side of the field. The other team will follow him. But before crossing the line of scrimmage, the runner flips the ball backward to the quarterback. The quarterback can then throw it to an open receiver."

"We haven't practiced this!" Nico said. "How can we possibly do it during a game?"

Kat smiled. "You can do it because the MVP Club practiced it the other day!" she said.

The players looked at each other. They didn't know what to say.

"Um, Kat? Nico's right. We've never tried the flea flicker play. Maybe you need to rest for a bit," Luke said. "I can call Mom if you're not feeling well."

Kat shook her head. "We haven't practiced the flea flicker, but when we were moving all those balls for Ms. Suraci

a few days ago, we actually practiced all the *moves* for the play! Remember how Alice grabbed balls out of the closet and tossed them back to you, Nico? Then you threw them down the hall to Max, and Luke put them in the room. It's exactly the same thing. And we practiced it for over an hour!"

Nico thought about it. Then he clapped his hands. "You're right!" he said. "Great idea, Kat. Let's do it. It's our only chance."

FOOTBALL MVP

Franklin took the field. Nico called out the snap count.

"Blue sixty-two. Green thirteen. Red bed," Nico called out. "Hut, hut, hike!"

Max snapped the ball back to Nico.

The Hamilton defense counted to five-Mississippi and rushed toward Nico as he dropped back. Nico handed the ball to Alice. Max ran far off to the left. He moved past Logan as Logan was trying to follow Alice.

Alice took the ball and zipped to

the right. The Hamilton offense fol-
lowed her. As she was about to hit the
sideline, Alice tossed the football back
to Nico.

Before the Hamilton offense could
adjust, Nico grabbed the ball and cocked

his arm back. He spotted Max way down the field. As the Hamilton players tried to head for Nico, he flung his arm forward. The ball sailed out of his hand and arced down the field.

Max was wide open!

It was too late for Hamilton to recover and get someone to block the pass. Max just had to catch the ball! The crowd on the sidelines gasped. The field fell silent. The ball spiraled through the air.

Max was yards from the Hamilton end zone when the ball dropped into his hands. He tucked it between his hand and his elbow and darted forward.

Touchdown!

Max spiked the football.

The whistle blew. The game was over.

Franklin had won! They had beat Hamilton for the first time in years!

The Franklin football team cheered. Nico did a cartwheel. Alice and Luke high-fived each other. Kat danced around on the sidelines with her clipboard over her head. The other players on the team chanted, "Go, Franklin! Go, Franklin! Go, Franklin!"

Max picked up the football and started to jog back to the bench. But then he spotted a group of Hamilton players. They were directly between him and the rest of the Franklin team. The Hamilton players were moving together toward Max, and Logan was in the middle.

Max slowed down. He considered darting to the left or right, but before he could decide, Logan jogged up and stopped in front of Max.

Max's hands tightened on the football. "The game is over, Logan," he said. "We won."

Logan reached out his hand toward Max.

Max stepped back. Logan took a step forward. He reached out his hand again and grabbed Max's hand, then shook it.

"Yeah, I know the game is over," Logan said. "I just wanted to say that you played a good game. You really got me back there when you went through my legs. I should have focused on football instead of teasing you. Sorry. Sometimes I try so hard to be tough."

Max stared at Logan, and then shook his hand back. "Thanks," he said. "It's okay. You're a good player, too."

Logan pulled his hand away and then held up his fist. He waited for Max to make a fist, then Logan bumped his fist down on top of Max's like he was hitting a nail with a hammer.

"Next year!" he said with a smile. "We'll do it again. Same time, same place. But this time maybe I'll focus on football, so don't think you're going to win twice in a row!"

Max nodded. "You're on!"

Logan headed back to his side of the field. Max jogged over to join the rest of the Franklin team.

"Way to go, Max!" Kat called.

Max raised the football and tossed it to Nico. "It was Nico's pass that did it," he said.

Kat held up the book. "But it was

your trick play idea that saved the day," she said. "You also tied the game by rolling under Logan's legs. That was the perfect way to get back at him!"

Luke took the book from Kat's hands. He quickly flipped through the pages. He stabbed his finger at a page near the end and cried out, "Ah-ha! This is what I was looking for! This is the perfect trick play for right now."

"What do you mean? The game is over!" Max said.

Luke pretended to read the page quickly. "It's called icecreamarooski. According to the book, it's hard to say but easy to do. 'To execute an icecreamarooski, the entire football team should proceed at once to the nearest ice cream parlor. Once there, each member of the team should order a cone, cup, or sundae of their choosing!'"

"I'm in!" Nico said.

Luke said, "Me too. As long as we don't have to get peas on top of the ice cream!"

Alice, Kat, and the rest of the football team broke out in laughter.

After putting away their equipment, the team headed to Annabelle's. It took a little while for the whole team to order, but soon they were sitting in front of the store, slurping and scooping their way through their treats.

When they were done, Nico and Alice disappeared inside. When they came out a few minutes later, Nico was carrying something behind his back. Alice nodded to Kat.

Kat stood up and rapped her knuckles on the picnic table for attention. "As coach of the Franklin football team, I'd like to say we all did a great job today," she said. "We didn't give up when we were down, and we believed

in ourselves enough to come back and win the game!"

The entire team cheered.

Kat continued. "But we also wanted to recognize someone who really helped us with the win by finding new ways to play smarter and not just harder. That's why we're giving the MVP Club's first Football MVP Medal to Max!"

The team cheered again as Nico presented Max with a "medal" made out of a paper ice cream dish with a ribbon poked through it to hang around his neck. Alice had even used a small squirt of hot fudge sauce to write the words *Football MVP* in the center of the dish!

Max hung the medal around his neck. As he was doing it, his finger smudged one of the hot-fudge letters.

Max held up the messy finger and then put it in his mouth. He pulled it out with a pop!

A big smile crossed Max's face. "I have to say, that's the sweetest MVP medal I've ever tasted!"

MVP
Stats

Football

FOOTBALL TEAMS. Football teams have eleven players on the field at a time. But teams have many more players than that, because they can swap players in and out. NFL teams can have fifty-three players on them! Most teams have three special groups of players.

SPECIAL TEAMS. Special teams are used for kicking plays. A kicker tries to kick the ball for field goal attempts. Punters kick the ball on a fourth down.

LINE OF SCRIMMAGE. The line of scrimmage is the imaginary line that runs across the field where the ball is placed before a play. Neither team can cross over it before a play starts.

FIRST DOWN. A team has four tries (downs) to move the ball forward ten yards or to score. If a team doesn't move the ball forward ten yards by the end of the fourth down, the other team gets the ball. Flag football games can have a different number of downs and yards.

END ZONE. Football teams are aiming for the opponent's end zone. The end zone is an area between the end of the football field (the end line) and the goal line, where the goalpost is.

KICKOFF. Football games start with a kickoff. Kickoffs are when one team kicks the football to the other team. The other team tries to catch it and run down the field with it. Kickoffs also happen after the half and before each overtime. Flag football games usually don't have kickoffs.

SCORING. Touchdowns are when a team runs or passes the ball into the other team's end zone. A touchdown is worth six points. A field goal happens when a team kicks a football through the goalpost at the end of the field. Field goals are worth three points.

SUPER BOWL. The Super Bowl is football's championship game. It's the final game of the NFL season and is played on a Sunday in late January or early February, so it's known as Super Bowl Sunday.

SNAP. When a center (one of the offensive linemen) tosses the ball back to the quarterback at the start of a play, it's called a snap. Usually they throw it back to the quarterback from a bent-over position. But they don't have to throw it. It's legal for them to hand it off or even roll it!

OFFENSIVE POSITIONS. The offense plays when a team has the ball. It's their job to move the ball forward and score. Offensive linemen try to block the other team from reaching the quarterback. Backs and receivers run or catch passes. It's the quarterback's job to receive the ball on the snap and throw it, run with it, or hand it off.

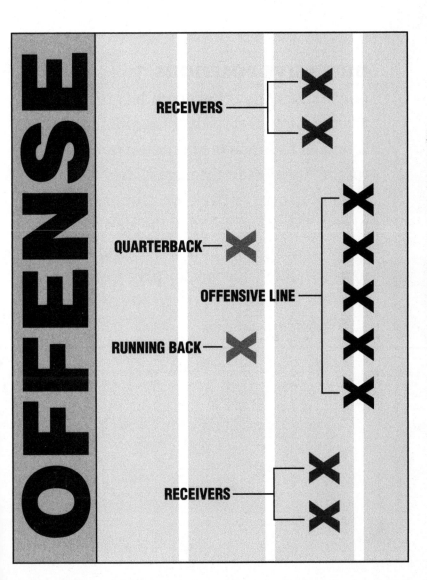

OFFENSE

RECEIVERS

QUARTERBACK

OFFENSIVE LINE

RUNNING BACK

RECEIVERS

DEFENSIVE POSITIONS. The defense plays when the other team has the ball. It's their job to stop the other team from scoring. Defensive linemen are closest to the line of scrimmage. They try to rush the quarterback or stop running plays. Linebackers play behind them. They try to stop runners or intercept passes. Defensive backs play even farther back. They also try to stop runners and intercept passes.

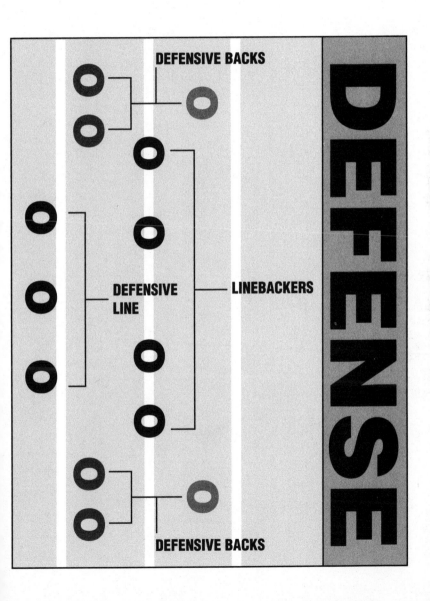

DEFENSIVE BACKS

DEFENSIVE LINE

LINEBACKERS

DEFENSIVE BACKS

DEFENSE

Turn the page for a sneak peek at

TWEET! A whistle pierced the sound of bouncing basketballs. It was Ms. Suraci, the school's PE teacher and basketball coach. She walked into the gym carrying a clipboard and a backpack.

The MVP Club and all the other teams gathered around her. Ms. Suraci blew her whistle again and waved her clipboard in the air for quiet.

"We've got a busy basketball season this year," she said. "Our first travel tournament is this weekend. It's the Big City Basketball Blowout. The playoff game on Wednesday will decide whether the red team or the blue team goes this weekend. But we have lots of other tournaments scheduled, so all the teams will have a chance to travel."

The kids clapped. A chant of *"Red Team! Red Team! Red Team!"* rose up from Jenna and the members of her team. Ms. Suraci waved the clipboard for quiet again.

"Listen, no one will be going anywhere unless we can raise some extra money for travel expenses," she said. Ms. Suraci leaned over and reached into her backpack. "And here's how we're going to do it."

She held up a shiny bag of popcorn. "We're having a fund-raiser for our travel teams," she said. "The school's parent group has donated all this popcorn. You each need to sell as much popcorn as you can by the end of the week in order to have enough money for this year's tournaments."

Ms. Suraci opened a couple of bags of popcorn and passed them around. Everyone grabbed a few bites and chomped away.

"Mmm . . . this is good," Kat whispered to Alice. "I'll take some more!"

"What do we get if we sell the popcorn?" Tim Reagan on the gold team asked.

"Good question," Ms. Suraci asked. "You get to play travel basketball!"

Everyone laughed.

Ms. Suraci rustled around in her backpack. "But we do have prizes, based on how much each team sells," she said. "The team that sells the second-most popcorn wins five of these." She held up a bright-green T-shirt. It had pictures of popcorn all over it.

"Wow!" said some of the kids.

"Neat," Max whispered to Alice.

"But the team that sells the *most* popcorn wins these!" Ms. Suraci said. She held up a bright-green sweatshirt that read *FRANKLIN BASKETBALL*.

"I want that," Luke said.

"But that's not all," Ms. Suraci said. "The *person* on the winning team who sells the most popcorn gets the grand prize!" She reached into the backpack and lifted up the coolest pair of sneakers the kids had ever seen. They had special black-and-silver soles, with red stripes running up the sides.

"Oh man, that's great!" Peter Paterson from the purple team said. "Those look *fast!*"

"Hey, those are the brand-new ones that just came out," a boy said.

"The winner of the contest will get a pair in his or her size," Ms. Suraci said. "Tom's Sneaker Store on Main Street is donating them. I wish we had enough for a whole team, but we don't. If you want to win the sneakers, your *team* has to sell the most popcorn compared to other teams, and *you* have to sell the most popcorn on your team."

The kids all rushed forward to

inspect the sneakers and shirts. Max held up a T-shirt. "That would look great on you," Kat said. Nico picked up a sneaker. It felt super light in his hands.

TWEET! Ms. Suraci blew her whistle again. "Follow me!" she called. She led everyone to her office. Ms. Suraci had a huge pile of pop-corn bags in the corner.

"Everyone starts with thirty," she said. "But if you need more, stop in and see me."

Ms. Suraci handed out the larger bags full of single-serving popcorn packages. Each team stepped forward to get their popcorn, then ran outside to start selling it. The MVP Club's blue team was last.

As soon as they got their popcorn, Max and Alice headed for the front door.

"Hang on," Nico called. "Not so fast!"

The MVP Club looked at Nico.

"Why not?" Alice asked. "We've got to start selling."

Nico waved his hand in the direction of the gym at the end of the hallway. "We *will*, but first, we should practice for half an hour," he said. "After all, now we've got the gym to ourselves! And we need more practice before Wednesday's game if we're going to win." A big empty gym was one of Nico's favorite places to be in the whole world.

"Ugh!" Luke groaned. "Practice, shmactice! Everyone is out selling popcorn, and we're not!"

"Yes, but we'll be the ones winning the game on Wednesday and heading to the Big City Basketball Blowout this weekend!" Nico said. "It will be worth it. We'll still have time to sell popcorn later. Come on!"

Nico led the MVP Club back down the hall to the gym. But as they got closer, they could hear that the gym wasn't empty! Someone was shooting baskets.

"Hey, who's that?" Nico said. "I thought everyone was gone!"

Nico ran to the doors of the gym and pulled them open. The MVP Club burst inside.

On the far side of the gym, there was a boy shooting baskets.

"Hey, what are you doing here?" Max called out.

The boy grabbed the ball and swung around. He stared at the members of the MVP Club for a moment.

Then he dropped the ball and took off running!

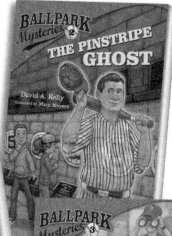

Get ready for more baseball adventure!

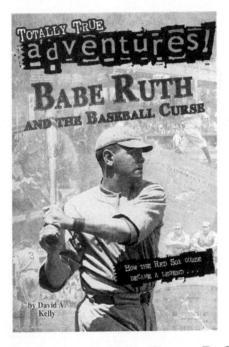

Did Babe Ruth curse the Boston Red Sox
when he moved to the New York Yankees?

Available now!

New friends. New adventures.
Find a new series . . . just for you!

FOR THE SPORTS FAN

FOR THE ADVENTURER

FOR THE SUPERSTAR

FOR THE DREAMER

FOR THE ANIMAL LOVER

FOR THE EXPLORER

RandomHouseKids.com